The Fear Responses of a Union Iron Worker

Robert F. Nelson, Jr.

DEDICATION

This book is dedicated to:
...My parents who put up with me all my life;
...My brothers Bill, Terry and Tony;
...ALL my Union Iron Workers Family, Nate, Pop Tart, Billy T. etc.
...and to ALL Union Brothers & Sisters from A-Z
(you get the picture; we are talking about everyone... Boilermakers, Operators, Electricians, Carpenters...) and Jimmy Tuck (R.I.P)

It is because of your support and encouragement that I continue to write!

Bob Nelson

CONTENTS

The Fear Responses of a Union Iron Worker

And Samson said unto them,

Though ye have done this,

yet will I be avenged of you

and after that I will cease.

Judges 15:7
KJV Holy Bible

FORWARD

Robert F. Nelson, Jr. is a raw, reflective gritty writer, that draws you into his stories and characters with your eyes wide-shut! His writing reflects the fearless voice of humanity from a segment of the population that is often stereotyped and limited to the boundaries of our choices within the human condition. In our society, we help to create and/or perpetuate conditions that force the emergence of the heroes and the villains that populate systems like prisons, jails, government and business. Nelson's eclectic mix of characters reflect shadows of his past choices and experiences while revealing the lessons learned in his struggle for redemption and his place in our place in society. The echoes of Nelson's life, for more than 35 years, are steeped in the blood, sweat and tears of a unionized worker. The intelligence, confidence and fearlessness needed to breathe among Union Iron Workers is not fit for just anyone--- as is the writing of this genre of stories.

Nelson was born in Chicago, Illinois at a time in the late 60's when grifters, metal cars, and impetuous youth reigned over urban neighborhoods; he was part of the band that often-carved career pathways narrowed by jail, drugs, or both. Nelson's journey began to shape his youthful impetuousness of being invincible. An identical twin, Nelson and his twin brother were both diagnosed early in life with Dyslexia. Coping through their learning difference by developing their own language, would eventually become part of the long-term impact inspiring his creative expressive writing. Learning to read and write by the dedication of his mother, Nelson also became keen in the skill of observation. Growing up in the 70's and 80's, life presented many hard lessons. But one important lesson learned by high school is that time is a commodity and he would make the best of it- even if it cost him. Each lesson, became an artistic reminder added to his collection of tattooed epithets and iconography amassing his body as proof of his dedication to the American Iron Worker experience.

By 16, Robert now "Bobby", knew he was ready to venture on his own to start his next adventure of life. A chapter that cultivating a plan leading him to attaining his GED and first real job as a union window washer. His fearlessness allowed him to work at heights most would never endeavor on scaffolding, suspension chairs and descenders. This work was a natural foundation to his work as a Union Iron Worker on bridges, high rises, and skyscrapers. Fearless at heights unknown, but when his feet planted squarely on the ground, faced the realities of life as a loner and drifter. Following the call of the seasons and the growing metropolis he was always able to find work and a decent brawl. Not because he started trouble but because he never backed down from it. This pattern of turmoil and redemption landed him in many of the jails and prisons that inspired his writing. A legal mind, and shaped by his understanding of the penal system and the law, he shared his knowledge, legal rights, and skill helping others. Help took the form of teaching others their legal rights and often by default to read and write.

Reflections of the characters in his stories echo personalities and the depth of the imagery needed to colorfully frame each story. The way that each story draws you in, forces you to find the personality traits of someone you know too, maybe all too well! The protagonists in his stories are often rough and rugged, no excuses, loners who through loyalty, living their truth (even when on the edge) are finding redemption or places that they belong. If you like to know what motivates the male mind, or what types of women peak his interest (and why) this interesting perspective of this garden variety may give you just the glimpse you need!

Heather Hetheru, is a published author and Personal Change Coach, with an understanding of the human condition and the world that can be found and lost in expressive writings. Editor and co-writer of more than 35 publications, she was taken by the colorful and edgy writing of Robert F. Nelson, Jr. As a writer, she sees this collection as the first of many adventures to come by this talented writer and story teller.

The Fear Responses of a Union Iron Worker

Let it Be Known:

Skilled Labor Ain't Cheap

&

Cheap Labor

Ain't Skilled.

THE FEAR RESPONSES
OF A UNION IRON WORKER

At first blush, the "proud to be a Union Ironworker" presents himself as an audacious and attitudinal anthropocentric adventurous alpha-male. These perceptions would be well founded because they are 100% true and correct! In popular culture, the Union Ironworker is properly viewed as he is depicted—the last of a daring and dying breed; the "Cowboy of the Skies" (with good reason). Because he is! For most people, Cowboys instantly invoke images of a host of things as well as conditions that no longer exist in the politically correct, emasculated, overly sensitive and feminized climate that now permeates modern American society. Cowboys portray the wide-open range – FREEDOM- gunfighters like John Wayne and the iconic Marlboro Man. Union Ironworkers epitomize the values that Americans who have not succumbed to the siren call of the Almighty Dollar hold near and dear; hard work, fear of God and love of family. The Union Ironworker believes in the ethos of Manifest Destiny. Without it, no bridge or skyscraper would have ever been built.

At second glance, it would appear that this belligerent badass hedonistic "he-man" who has stayed at the bar until "Last Call" at 2 am, with his fellows, boasting of his sexual prowess and conquests won't be making it into work this morning. "Work hard, play hard" is one of his guiding sentiments. It seems that even when he has overindulged in the later portion of this governing philosophy, that work might take second place to recovery. The Union Ironworker is not only going to make it to work –but he is going to be on time (because he will be there early in order to ensure that he is not late). In fact, he will be ready to work and if not sober… at least a reasonable approximation thereof. How is this humanly possible? Due to the unassailable fact that he is motivated by the most base, fundamental, and peremptory of all human emotions: FEAR.

How can the Union Ironworker; a veritable demi-god in his own right; experience any emotion even remotely akin to fear? Is this not the cowardly attribute to be found in lesser mortals such as carpenters, glaziers and hear and frost insulators? From time-to-time even a Union Ironworker will have a face-to-face encounter with Phobos and Deimos (the Gods of Fear and Terror). What separates the Union Ironworker from his lowly subordinates is how he reacts when confronted by danger or its counterparts fear and terror. Fortitude in the face of peril does not mandate an absence of fear but a mastery of self (or one portion of it at any rate).

It won't be an easy task but this particular Union Ironworker is going to change his current stagger back to his normal swagger… with the aid of his tavern wench and current flame who propels them through the deserted city streets at the wheel of a '95 Thunderbird SC. Yes! Union Ironworkers drive American-made sports cars with superchargers, twin turbos, duel cams, and five or six speed close-ratio manual gear boxes. They leave the "piece of shit" pick-up trucks for the likes of tin knockers, operator and boilermakers. If the bar maid's intent is to scare him sober by driving the SUPER COUPE at a rate of maximum velocity… she is doing, a superb job of it. Bear in mind that this personification of manly virtue who; regularly and routinely; plies his craft up in the clouds prowling the catwalk among the 6' tall letters of the alphabet spelling out:

A-M-B-A-S-S-A-D-O-R B-R-I-D-G-E

rarely ever ties off, unless it happens to be particularly breezy up there (just slightly over 530 feet above the Detroit River) is now doing something that he has NEVER done; hastily fastening his seatbelt with eyes clenched tightly shut as he screams at her to slow down. Her driving honestly scares him.

When the terrifying ten-minute trip is safely concluded and they are parked curbside in front of her house, the Union Ironworker opens the passenger door of the T-bird with a trembling hand. In an obscene and unseemly parody of a bulimic teenage girl, he disgorges $50.00 worth of booze and beer into the gutter. Once inside he spends an hour and a half alternating between ice-cold and scalding hot showers. He consumes several pots of the strongest and most vile coffee he has ever tasted... then he begins pounding down Rock Star, Monster and Red Bull energy drinks.

The Union Ironworker is highly motivated by FEAR. If he shows up late again, the Detroit International Bridge Company will terminate him from their employ. Even though he is a damn good worker he will be deemed unreliable and will be let go. The Steward has warned him. The Union Hall will get involved and he could be brought up on charges for violating the Union Ironworker Standards of Excellence and be subjected to a hefty fine. With no job... there is no money for the high-octane premium fuel that the T-Bird absolutely positively requires... or the full coverage insurance... or the clutch the Gin Mill Goddess may have just smoked. At present, the only thing the Union Ironworker fears about recovery is that it won't be speedy enough of one. And at the moment, it is a bad thing which perversely is a good thing. The Union Ironworker does not thrive on danger--- but he does not shrink from it either. The FEAR makes him stronger, because he draws strength and resolve from his two favorite Bible verses: Psalms 82:6 "I have said Ye are gods..." and John 10:34 "... I said, Ye are gods..."

---THE END---

VALUES CLARIFICATION

The 1986 Ford Thunderbird aero coupe had been parked alongside of the weathered ramshackle turn-of-the-(2oth) century barn for at least five years that I knew about. It was Ford blue and rusting away at the bottoms of the doors and rockers and also the front fenders and rear quarters were pretty rough. I had seen it many times and had always intended to stop and make an inquiry but never did because I was always doing something more pressing. Then one spring morning I did stop because I saw people going into the house. I had and still do have a 1985 30th anniversary T-bird. The 1983 to 1986 aero coupe body style is no longer a presence in the junk yards of SW Michigan – or elsewhere- I needed parts.

A man answered my knock. He had the build and demeanor of an ex-convict and brawny arms covered with some of the crudest jailhouse ink I've ever seen. It was like gawking at the scene of an accident or in this case a crime scene… it was so appalling and yet so mesmerizing I could hardly tear my eyes away… Was that supposed to be a woman or a Pitbull with a rack? And that thing on his chest… was it a pinwheel…or maybe a flower of some sort---it was neither---it was a backward swastika I realized.

"Hi. I'm wondering about the '86 T-bird. Is it for sale" I asked. "You see a for sale sign on it Sport?" said the tattooed behemoth. "Vern, don't be an asshole!" A woman's voice shrieked form the interior of the house. "See what he's willing to offer!" Vern peered at me intently and I realized that he was examining my tattoos. "I got all my tats in jail." He announced proudly.

Clearly. I thought to myself. "I got a couple while I was locked up." However, unlike with Vern, the guy who inked me did not have more ambition than actual ability. "I've done time in the Michigan Department of

Corrections." Vern boasted. **<u>Ahhh an Icebreaker</u>**. Not something I would normally volunteer to a perfect stranger – even a tattooed one. But, when in Rome… "Me too. I got my number in 1989. I did 10 years –mostly in max." "I was in level 1 and the camps." Vern replied.

"Vern!" The women shrieked again. "Don't be an asshole! Invite the man inside! Offer him something to drink!" Vern pushed the screen door open with a meaty forearm and stood aside for me to pass through. "C'mon inside Sport." I stepped into the bleak musty interior of the living room and when my eyes adjusted to the gloom. I ascertained that I was in Vern's man cave which was part taxidermist studio with moth-eaten deer heads on the walls, a rather scrofulous owl with outstretched wings clutching on equally scabrous mouse in one set of talons and part music room with a battered drum kit and boxes of assorted junk stacked haphazardly through the room. The overall effect of the décor was early American Junkyard due to numerous milk crates full of car parts of unknown origin.

"Howzabout a brewsky Sport?" Vern stepped past me and went through a dining room. I saw a middle-aged lady seated at a home computer who looked up at me from the screen, waved languidly at me and then bellowed at Vern as he passed by her. "Don't be an asshole Vern! Just one beer now! You hear me?" "I can't help but hear you woman. Yer' ten feet away from me." It was quite obvious to me that rudimentary mathematics was not Vern's strong suit due to the fact that the distance separating them was more accurate at ten inches but I did not feel it was my place to comment.

Vern returned carrying two 40-ounce bottles of old Milwaukee. "She said only one beer." Vern leered as he handed me one. We clink bottles. Male conspirators united against Man's common enemy; a bossy woman. I wondered how anyone could drink such horse piss especially at 8:40 am. I was an Old-Style (brand of beer) man myself and never before 10 am. "I wondered about that car for years." I said. "I'm in town for a week before I go back to work in Gary, Indiana. So, when I saw you guys pull in I thought I would stop." "Sure." Vern agreed. "Let's go out and fire her up." I was incredulous. This was almost too good to be true, I thought. "You mean it runs?" I asked hoping my voice did not betray my excitement. "Oh yeah. Like a top, Sport. Sure does." He bragged.

We went outside with our beers and walked over to the T-Bird. Two of the tires were flat and all 4 severely weathered. The body was rough but not so far gone as to be unsalvageable. The interior was dirty but was in excellent shape. No burns, nicks or tears and a lovely shade of blue known as Corinthian Blue. It would look awesome cleaned up and transplanted into my '85. Not to mention all of those extra parts that were becoming increasingly harder to find and costlier. A running parts car! It made me giddy with joy.

Vern went into the barn and returned carrying a newish Sears Allstate battery. I pop the hood open. The engine was for the ubiquitous and venerable 3.8 V6 with 96,000 miles showing on the odometer. We installed the battery. The key was in the ignition. Vern got in, pumped the gas pedal a couple of times and the Bird roared to life. "I got $250 cash right now." I offered. "The hell you say, Buddy. This here is a racer." Vern slapped the front fender sending a cascade of rust, paint chips and dirt falling to the ground. "Solid as the day she rolled off the line. And the air conditioner blows ice cold." Racer? Air conditioner? Sacrilege! Never in the same breath! This was a basic 3.8 not 2.2 Turbo Coupe or a Super Coupe! I thought to myself. "Well... what would you take for it then?" I asked.

"Hmmm....Listen sport if you ain't gonna drink your beer---- I'll drink it."

I actually had not wanted the beer in the 1st place. I was driving my dad's truck that morning and it went without saying that there would be no drinking and driving. Not in the "Old Man's" truck. It boiled down to fundamental issues of respect and trust. It was all unspoken but I knew it. Every time he entrusted me with the use of one of his vehicles, it was law.

So I handed over the beer to Vern who drained it in one mighty drought followed by a belch of equally epic proportions and a bleary grin as if pleased to convey what was becoming readily apparent. An astute observation on the part of his conscionable better half: Vern was an asshole. "Tell you what Sport. She runs and has a clear title. You gimme the $250 cash and do some digging for me and I keeps my battery for the car sounds like a good deal?" He stared.

"Digging?" I questioned. "Digging. From the North East corner of the house 3 feet down for 50 yards to them there Birch trees. Gotta be at least 2 feet wide for the drain for my sump system." He gestured. We shook on it. The ground was soft and damp. A couple days digging at best. I calculated the cost of the car at roughly $700 between my labor and the cash. A running parts car with an immaculate interior, factory tinted glass and ice-cold air. For digging a ditch? How bad could it be?

Bad. Very bad. I thought about giving up 2 hours into it the first morning. But I had shook on it. We had made a deal. Vern and I had an oral agreement---- something every convict an ex-convict can understand. A point of principle that needs no pontification. The ground was soft and yielding. Deceptively so, those first 6 to 8 inches. Vern did not provide shovels. I broke 2 of the spades I borrowed from my dad. I was digging precisely in the course that Vern charted for me in orange spray paint on the grass. I had located an underground asteroid belt. Also, the telephone line and a power line that ran out to the barn. It took me 4 and a half days of backbreaking labor to dig the trench for the placement of the PVC drain tile with a pick axe. I unearthed enough rock to use for the foundation of a house as well as a new found respect for union and non-union laborers alike.

When I was finished with my contractual obligation, I knocked on the door of the house and ask Vern for the title to the T-Bird. He gave me that unblinking stare of a basilisk. "Can't seem to locate it, Sport. I looked----" Wham! Wham! The lady came up behind Vern and began beating him over the head with a broom. "Vern! Don't be an asshole! I told you I won't stand for you to cheat this man after he works so hard for us!" Vern fled past me and ran into the barn. "The title is in the glove box Mister. Vern told me so hisself. I apologize for my brother. He was taught better. Ma always said he has a devil in him."

I drove that T-Bird for 6 months before it threw a rod. Out of all the cars I've owned it was the one I worked the hardest for and valued the most.

---THE END---

BUYING A WHORE

So, the Most Expensive Whore I've ever bought is my ex-wife. Bitch will get $815.00 a month outta my pension when I retire in 14 years. Gold-digging bitch. Unlike a lot of men who "claim" they never pay for it... I do and make no bones about it. I feel that I am making a contribution: you know what I mean? Like doing something good and positive for society. I am "making an impact." Some people get a warm fuzzy feeling in the cockles of the heart when they donate blood. Me? I get a warm fuzzy deep down in my balls when I blow a load down the gullet of a hot ass hooker wearing a dayglo pink miniskirt after I've successfully negotiated "the ironworker discount" for myself and a couple buddies. I'm doing social work: supporting single working moms and the guys who say they don't pay to get a shot of guts are like the guys who claim they don't jagoff: LIARS or sexually repressed serial masturbators. Or...theses mother fuckers ain't never been married or they are Queer.

I've bought whores since I was 16 and NEVER not one fucking time ~LITERALLY~ have I ever regretted my fucking time with a whore. I cannot say the same with the respect to my ex-wife and the institution of marriage. Nowadays a man can actually be charged with "Spousal Rape" for taking what is his by right (not to mention the reason the mother fucker got married in the first place: unlimited 24-7 access to the rod oven). You ever hear of whores being raped? How do you rape a hooker? At best/worst, you get charged with robbery if you fail to pay.

In my career as a Union Ironworker, I've worked in 39 states and I don't know…probably 200+ cities. And I can personally attest that any place I've been with a population of three or more, there is a whorehouse, a dope house and a blind pig where a working man can get what he wants~when he wants. Pronto.

Escort Service girls, and porn stars in Vegas cash my paychecks. They front me cash when I'm tapped, bail me out of jail, pack me lunches and take me to work. It's better than being married: I don't have to talk to them, kiss them or put up with any lip~except for the lip service I like. Unlike in marriage, I GET WHAT I PAY FOR. There is no "not tonight I have a headache" with your friendly neighborhood prostitute. It's all about me. When I want it. How I want it. In my humble opinion: Prostitution should be legalized yesterday and unionized! From the Brooklyn Bridge to the Oakland Bay Bridge. There should be a set standardized price just like buying a pair of No. 877 boots from any Red Wing boot store coast-to-coast. $250.00 out the door and 10% off if you show your union card.

The reality is this: Prostitution is the World's Oldest Profession. It is an industry. I've never had any STD from a hooker (I don't have unprotected sex with the broads). In fact…I can honestly state unequivocally that the riskiest sexual behavior I've ever engaged in was having unprotected sex with my high school sweetheart slut that I married. I thank God ALMIGHTY on a daily basis that the pig did not contaminate me with some incurable infectious fungus. She has toxic pussy. It should be designated by the EPA????

Needless to say, my penchant for prostitutes has caused me [ahem] problems from time-to-time. Some minor, others not so minor. For example: in Omaha Local 21 IW territory, one day my bro Willis called me and told me "Be out front. I will pick you up in ten minutes."

"What's up?" I asked.

"All the people from New Orleans, displaced by Katrina are being housed at the old Civic Center. Let's go scope out the bitches."

We did. The "Ho Stroll" was packed with pussy. Like a can of sardines. The first broad was offended because I tried to get her to blow us both for $25.00. "You must think Imma crack ho." She said in an aggrieved tone.

"I dunno what your substance abuse issue is Miss." I replied. "but in your reduced circumstances and the market fluctuation due to the glut of yet more hos into Omaha… surely you can see that in order to be competitive in this over saturated market—"

"Look bitch", Willis is Black and spoke the lingo a little more blunt and terse than I… "Is you gonna whip some skull on us for $25.00 or is you not?! If not piss off! You is a ho."

* * *

Another time in Omaha... no sooner do I peel a beautiful redhead hooker off the street in front of the Salvation Army Homeless Shelter before I even got a chance to see if the carpet matches the drapes... Damn The Bad Luck!!! A OPD Black and White lights me up with the cherries and berries. An older cop comes up to me on the driver's door of my F250 Super Duty and a young cop with a pugnacious attitude goes to the passenger door. You can always tell the cop with the attitude. Typically young, White and something to prove. The fingerless black leather gloves and the Bat Man utility belt are dead giveaways. This one clearly used Sean Penn in Colors as his role model.

Old Cop: Ya know ya got a known prostitute in the vehicle son.

Me: No Sir. I have no idea what occupation this young lady has. She asked me to give her a ride to the Circle K Store. So, I'm giving her a ride.

Old Cop: Mm hmm. [I pass him my license, insurance and registration cards] I'll bet. A ride huh...

Young Cop: What's all this? Gestures at all the holes poked into my headliner from the stiletto heels of the distaff. There is one black hi-heel still stuck in the headliner over the backseat of my crew cab.

Me: My wife did all that (I lie).

Old Cop: Get out Elektra. I know you got warrants.

Young Cop: We are gonna let you go…. This time, but if we catch you buying a whore, we will arrest you, impound your truck and your name will be in the Police Blotter in the newspaper.

Me: Buddy, if you catch me buying a whore, you can put my smiling face on that billboard right there.

The young cop glared at me. The old cop did what you're doing. Laughed and laughed.

---THE END---

FACES

After you do time with a guy for several years—like it or not—eventually you're going to hear his life story. Not once, but many times. In my pal Hot Wire's case, his whole life story revolves around the six weeks of heavenly bliss he spent with a dame named Amie.

His normally stoic face would <u>almost</u> (but not quite) become animated as he subjected me (for the umpteenth time) to the long, drawn-out, and extremely boring digression of the time he and Amie—the love of his life—were in the family room at his parents' home. They were engaged in America's favorite pastime-watching a rental video (Prizzi's Honor). He turned to Amie and declared his undying love (and presumably honorable intentions). He requested to kiss her and then permission granted, he proceeded to do so (undoubtedly with great ardor).

It was not hard for me to conjure up visions of an infatuated (and pussy whipped) Hot Wire—slavishly devoted to his darling Amie; holding doors, fetching and carrying, lighting her cigarettes, kissing her hands (and her ass) gallantly; ready and willing to appease her every whim—as I feigned interest and suffered through the equally monotonous and oft- repeated extensively detailed accounts of the two times Amie invited him to her parents' house for dinner; Who was there and what they said. The floral pattern of the china. The seating arrangements. What was served (rabbit and venison respectively). The best damned cooking he ever had and the most deliciously aromatic descriptions I've ever heard or smelled. Yes, I could smell it!

Amie this. Amie that. Her mother is a Saint. Her father is the nicest guy you would ever want to meet. Her sister is sweetness personified. Amie is <u>so</u> intelligent (she made the Dean's list). Amie is a loving, caring, sensitive, kind, warm, generous person—a veritable angel (she sent Hot Wire a Christmas card…. <u>Seven</u> years ago.)

Hot Wire had Amie up on a pedestal and if he peeked up her skirt as probably was his wont, he kept that part to himself. Unlike the overwhelming majority of prisoners, aside from the now-ingrained story of the "first-kiss" with Amie. Hot Wire has <u>never</u> discussed nocturnal affairs and the not infrequent yard-bird sessions of sexual conquests seemed to offend him greatly.

I'll never forget the time when a group of us cons were huddled over a card table inspecting the charms of the latest <u>Penthouse</u> centerfold. Strolling along Hot Wire approached—and upon realizing what it was that commanded our undivided attention—he let out a quick choke and his hands flew up to his face, covering his eyes. Then, peeking at the Monthly Queen of Daydreams through splayed fingers, he announced deadpan, "Amie is much hotter", and strode off.

It's been well over two years since Hot Wire mentioned the

name "Amie" in any context. Fact is, he ain't said much to anyone. I believe it has finally sunk in that what he feels for Amie is not reciprocal. She lives a mere 30-minute drive from here and hasn't visited him since 1989. On several occasions I've been sorely tempted to go over a strike up a conversation. Instead, I keep my distance. We are long-time friends, but as one large inmate recently observed of Hot Wire, "that look on his face makes him totally unapproachable."

---THE END---

FASTER THAN YOU'LL EVER LIVE TO BE

"Your best bet is to just head on over to the bank, get the reward money and ride out of town. Mr. Hines. The Clemens boys have a lot of friend around these parts." Sheriff Jeb Baldwin advised nervously as he handed Charlie Hines the chit for the $1,000.00 bounty on horse thieves Matt and Mike Clemens, who had been wanted dead or alive in Missouri, Illinois, Indiana and Michigan. Hines had brought both brothers in dead.

"They <u>had</u> a lot of friends." Hines corrected and tucked the voucher into the pocket of his tattered homespun linen shirt. "I'll be in town a couple of days. Long enough to get some hot grub, good whiskey and a bad woman. Any friends of the Clemens' who come gunnin' for trouble will get aplenty." With that Hines turned smartly on his heel—the heels of his boots were rundown and like him, had seen much better days --- and strode out of the Sheriff's office.

"Goddamned bounty hunters." Sheriff Baldwin grumbled humorlessly and watched from his window as Hines brusquely shouldered his way through the crowd of curious onlookers which had gathered out in front of Fennville, Michigan's small, solidly built stone jail to gape at the corpses of the Clemens' slung over their stolen mounts tied at the hitching rail. The Clemens' were attracting far more flies than men, and Baldwin downright resented the task that lay ahead of him which entailed leaving the jail's cool interior, going out into the midday heat and facing the swam of flies (and smell of sun bloated bodies) which would accompany him all the way to the undertaker's parlor.

Hines untied his valise from the saddle horn, pulled his Winchester and shotgun from their boots, draped his saddlebags over his shoulders and crossed the dusty street to The Soiled Dove saloon. Hines assumed from the name it was a watering hole in more than the conventional sense and thought it was one helluva clever moniker, he hoped he would have time for a bath and a soiled dove before he had to kill anyone. He knew it was inevitable that some outraged kin to, or friend of, the Clemens' would feel compelled out of some misguided sense of duty and honor to get themselves killed by calling him out. He would be forced to oblige them and add yet another tale to the growing legend of Charlie Hines: Bounty hunter and gunslinger.

He'd heard tell that some pulpwriter in Chicago had went and done a dime novel about him (which he had no inclination to read) after he had run the Sisson Bunch to ground in Albuquerque and took them back to Kansas City desiccated and stinking. Hines always brought his bounty in dead. The trouble of taking care of some desperado eager to avoid his fate with the hangman, who would drygulch him at the first opportunity was not worth the few hundred extra dollars more he would make from a warm body rather than a cold one.

After reading what that newspaperman Buntline immortalized about Wyatt Earp had been enough to sour Hines on books. Folks had taken to thinking Earp to be a genuine hero instead of the corrupt yellow belly backshooting coward he really was.

Pausing at the batwing doors of The Soiled Dove, Hines looked down at the pickinanny seated on top of an overturned keg, who stared in utter fascination at his big .44 caliber Navy model revolver-walnut grips worn down smooth as satin- resting in the cut down holster hanging low tied to his right hip. The boy then gazed up at him with eyes as big as saucers. Hines said with a barely suppressed chuckle; "Spout, there's a silver dollar in my pocket with your name on it to take that sorrel mare over there in front of the hoosegow down to the livery stable on the east end of town. I'm right particular about that hoss so give her a double measure of oats and rub her down real good." He flipped a dollar to the lad who caught it, abandoned his perch from the keg and darted across the street to collect the horse. "Tell the man at the stable I'll be down later to see to the bill." Hines called after the boy then stepped through the doors of The Soiled Dove and stopped to take in the measure of the place with a sweep of obdurate flint hard eyes.

There was a momentary lull in conversation as everyone stopped to look at him and then hurriedly away. The room held some ten tables, two of which were currently in use. One was occupied by several fellows who looked to be farmhands judging by their bib overalls, straw hats and cow flop covered boots. The other by four gents playing poker. Some well-to-do types in frock oats jawed it up with a bored looking fat man standing behind the bar polishing glasses. Some right pretty doves were clustered by a player piano.

Hines set his gear on top of an empty table. As he crossed the room to take a spot at the long fancy bar, conversation resumed in a considerably more subdued fashion. He caught hushed bits and piece over the jingle of his spurs.

"…Bounty hunter." "…gunslinger." "…killed them no account Clemens brothers…" "Charles Hines. Meaner than a sidewinder and twice as fast."

Mister, you'd be a mean sonuvabiatch too if you spent three years in the Indiana Reformatory and had to stand in line waiting for your turn to be whipped, Hines thought acidulously. He looked in the mirror hanging above the bar and hungrily eyed a pert brunette in a green velvet dress with plunging décolletage, who to his mind stood head and shoulders above the other girls clustered around the piano, until she flushed and looked away.

The fat, bored-looking glass polisher came down to Hines' end of the bar and introduced himself, "Howdy stranger. I'm Ed McKinny, proprietor of The Soiled Dove. What can I get you?" "Gimme a bottle of yer best whiskey. I also want a room, a bath and the gal there in the green dress." Hines pointed his trigger finger at the woman's reflection in the mirror. McKinny glanced over his should at the mirror and said briskly, "Jack Daniels is my best." He looked dubiously at Hines' ragged appearance. "At $4.00 a fifth. A room is $2.00 a night. A cold bath is $.50 cent and a hot bath is a buck. Eva goes for $10. Everything is cash up front. No credit or promises."

Hines handed McKinny a twenty-dollar gold piece. "Keep the change. I want a room for two nights and a hot bath. I'll have that bath first and then attend to Mr. Daniels and Eva."

Several hours later Hines felt like a new man after having wet his whistle with Old No. 7 brand sour mash; immersing himself in a galvanized tub of soapy water and a couple of leisurely dips in Eva's hot spring. When Hines woke up he disentangled himself from Eva's sleeping form, got out of the creaking brass bed and washed up from the pitcher and basin on the rickety table that was the only other piece of furniture in the room. He removed his one clean set of clothes from the valise and dressed. After strapping on his gun belt he gently shook Eva by the shoulder. She woke up and smiled at him.

"I'm going downstairs to find a card game. Be here where I get back." He pressed one of his last two $20 gold pieces into her hand. "That's yours. Don't give it to that pimp McKinny." She kissed him gratefully.

No sooner had Hines moseyed up to the bar and ordered a beer when a young mean looking cuss—who was the only other man in the room packing a sidearm beside himself--- bearing a very strong resemblance to the recently departed Clemens brothers--- at the other end of the bar said in a loud clear voice, "Bounty man, you killed my cousins today."

"Are you calling me out, boy?" "I am. My name is Clancy Clemens and I'm gonna kill you."

The men standing between them at the bar fled like a flock of startled deer to the other side of the room and McKinny disappeared behind the bar quicker than a prairie dog dropping into its den.

Hines downed his beer, wiped his mouth and looked over at Clemens, who wore two Colt peacemakers. Clemens' hands looked steady, his right hovered dangerously close above the butt of his six shooter.

Hines stepped back away from the bar and said coldly, "Slap leather." He allowed Clemens to completely clear his holster and then threw down, flinging cold death with the unerring accuracy of Zeus hurling a thunderbolt. He walked over to Clemens' body which twitched spasmodically in death throes, and retrieved his quivering Arkansas toothpick which had penetrated Clemens' left eye embedded to the hilt in what little brains Clemens had possessed.

Hines whirled around clawing for his pistol when he heard the sound of hammers cocked back. As soon as he spotted the sawed-off double barrel shotgun McKinny held aimed at his head with his peripheral vision he knew he was a goner. Suddenly, the sharp, distinctive crack of a 30/30 lever action sounded, and a hole erupting blood like a geyser appeared in the center of McKinny's forehead.

Hines looked up at Eva who stood naked as a jaybird, somewhat disheveled but no soiled dove she, at the head of the stairs with his smoking Winchester. She lowered the rifle slowly and said in a trembling voice, "He was going to shoot you."

Eva dropped the gun and dashed down the stairs---oblivious to the wide eyes-opened mouthed stares of the men in the bar--- threw herself into Hines arms and said, "I'm faster than you'll ever live to be. McKinny was my uncle on my Pa's side. He was my only kin and took me in when my folks died of the fever. He made me a whore. I hated him."

That's how bounty hunter and gunfighter Charles Hines, who went looking for a bad woman, came to hang up his guns---and knife---and marry the sweetest gal East of the Mississippi, half owner of The Soiled Dove saloon.

---THE END---

MORE WHORE STORIES

My best friend and road dog is Pop Tart, a Journeyman Ironworker out of Local No. 21 Omaha is best described like the breakfast food: "Crazy Good." I love the guy. Believe me: Anybody who bonds me out of jail for $5,000 cash and then again for $500 cash a week later has my complete and unswerving loyalty. The bail out-of-jail incident transpired during a bitter and acrimonious dissolution of marriage with the Most Expensive Whore I ever bought.

I rented Pop Tart's basement while I was in the process of transition from POW (Prisoner of Whore) to eligible bachelor taking home $1,800 a week like clockwork every Friday. We were both peering out the kitchen window, checking out a pert and perky blonde that worked as a dancer in a titty bar in downtown Omaha. Pop Tart spent most of his time and paycheck there. I had never seen the wench before as I was not allowed in the establishment because the year before my identical twin brother came to Omaha to work and managed to get himself barred from all the upscale establishments featuring frontal nudity. There was a God: as proof directly across the alley from us sunbathing in the tiniest thong imaginable lay the Delightful Destiny. I ran down to my room and fetched my binoculars so I could get a better look at the display. Hot damn! "Every man for himself" I told Pop Tart.

"Keep dreamin'." Pop Tart leered as he snatched the binoculars and handed me a Blatz beer. "I've gotta better chance than you at getting lucky cuz I been loading that g-string with dollar bills for three weeks." He drained his beer and left for his anger management session.

I would be pissed off and have serious anger problems too, if anything to do with not getting pussy... I pissed away all my hard-earned money on a bitch who never set out the pussy. Its why the Most Expensive Whore I ever bought and I divorced. If I do dream, I don't recall them. I'm not a gambler and unlike dreams, I don't recall luck having anything to do with getting pussy. I went across the alley and introduced myself to the Divine Destiny.

Two hours later down in my room the phone rings. I had both hands full so I put it on loud speaker. It was my Boss, Mike the Jew and he was extremely irate, to put in mildly. "You mother fucker! Don't tell me yer Dad died! I already called your mom and he is alive and well. Goddamnit! You beg me to put you on the Raising Gang and I do and then you don't show up for work. Sonofabitch! YOU better have a good reason why you ain't at work or yer fired! F-I-R-E-D: Fired! Come on! I wanna hear it! Or Else: Fired. What's the reason!?"

There was no point in telling him that Dad died if he already checked with Mom... I guess I had used that one too many times... I decided to come clean and tell the truth. Let the chips fall where they may.

ME: Do you hear that Boss?

Mike: Yeah. What is that?

ME: I'm getting a blowjob from the hooker across the alley.

Mike: The stripper PopTart has the hots for?!

ME: Yeah. Deck of smokes and a soda pop is the cost. Not a bad deal for a head job.

Destiny: Hey If You're gonna talk about me that a-way I'm leaving.

ME: Ah-ah-ah. We made a deal for these (I confiscated the 48 oz. fountain soda [Like a Big Gulp from 7-11] and the pack of generic menthol 100 smokes I had purchased for her at the Kum-n-Go in exchange for services rendered).

Mike: That's a good reason. Hurry the fuck up and get here!

Somerset, KY 2010 at a coal fire Power House

Me and Pop Tart are bouncing around on various gangs; Raising gang; Bolt-up; Rattle-up, doing whatever as needed. Mike the Jew is our Boss. We have lunch in his office every day. But one day, I skip lunch because I hooked up with a hooker in her Mazda in the parking lot. This all came about because I am an opportunist- especially when it comes to getting some pussy. I spent at this point in my life 12 years or so in prison and over six years being told "You're cut off" by the Most Expensive Whore I every bought during my farce of a marriage, so yeah, damned straight when the opportunity arises to participate in trench warfare I'm in it quick. I don't sit in the bars and piss away hard money on chippies tryna cadge free drinks. Fuck that. And despite having an extensive vocabulary (from taking full advantage of my free public-school education until I quite school in 1983 at age 16 so I could work iron, make money and travel about the Land of the Free/Home of the Brave (It's called autonomy). I try not to mince words:

> Buy you a drink? Hell no I won't. Why would I. For that matter: Why should I? Rude? The hell you say! Rude is sitting there in yer skimpy outfit, flashing yer long legs to me thinking thats a provocative hint of what might come if I buy you a drink is actually a drink-worthy proposition. Do you see gullible tattooed on my forehead!? Now if you want to give me a hand job: I will buy you a drink. And if you wanna join me in my Super Duty out in the parking lot and assume the position- don't be coy: You know damn well what position! Ankles behind the ears and I pound that pussy into quivering submission; I will buy you many drinks and give you $50 to boot.

All that sweet talk does is leave a man miserable and broke with blue balls. Women have all that hair down there for one thing and one thing only: to hide the hook! Wise up men! At any rate, earlier that morning in a diner we stopped at for breakfast this sweet looking broad cut into me for a smoke… She did not know how to smoke an unfiltered Chesterfield King without slobbering all over it so I bought her a pack of Marlboro lights out of the vending machine and copped a feel of those melons in exchange for my largess. I was encouraged when she gave me her phone number. Pop Tart, Philly Phil, Hoghead, Danny C and a couple other bros looked on from the table at the ongoing with pure envy. At 9:30 coffee break I called her and we arranged to meeting in the parking lot at lunch time to copulate like frenzied rabbits. And at lunch we did exactly that.

I made it back to Mike's office a few minutes before it was time to get back up on the iron. Mike said, "We missed you for lunch. Did you eat anything? What did you have for lunch?"

"A blow job." I replied, "Cost: $7.00 in smokes." "Hook me up." Pop Tart says, "I'll buy her a carton."

---THE END---

SUPER SOAKER

My eight year-old stepson, Tevon, and I were tooling along in my 1993 Thunderbird LX and there was an uncomfortable silence filling the car. Normally, he would be climbing in my lap, clamoring to be allowed to "drive" -- which consisted of him steering, however, he was angry with me because he felt – possibly and probably correctly – that I had just <u>unjustly</u> cuffed him upside the back of the head, for some minor infraction.

"Yeah… <u>That's Why You Smoke</u>!!" He growled with arms crossed as he glared at me indignantly.

<u>Uh Oh</u>, I thought worriedly as I put the T-Bird through it's paces and slid sideways through the driveway of the nearest parking lot which providentially happened to be a church. A sign from God or some sort of augury. A good place for soul-baring. <u>Rebellion-Time to nip this in the bud</u> – <u>Right now</u> – <u>before it gets out of hand.</u> The bird careened wildly for a moment when we came to a stop. My hands gripped the steering wheel tightly. Time for a man-to-man talk. Before the woman who ruled us both got involved.

"What? You wanna rat me out and tell mom that I started smoking again!? Okay. Fine. Go right ahead." I whipped out my cellphone and with feigned insouciance stiff-jabbed the buttons as I dialed my wife's cell phone number and then thrust the phone into his hands. "Just press the green send button to make the call to your mom."

He looked at me stonily, savoring the moment of holding complete sway over my fate, his finger hovering oh so menacingly above the green button and stopped in mid-descent when I hastily interposed, "But before you do… there's just one thing you need to know."

"What's that?" he leered, clearly enjoying my discomfiture. He had me over a barrel. We both knew it. When mom got the confirmation that I had resumed smoking and was lying to her on top of it [Gulp]… Well let's just say that our brief honeymoon phases would become even briefer: if not cease altogether. ☹

"**All** the extra-curricular activities, like driving this car, walking up to the Dairy Queen after dinner and them 'hugs all the way upstairs' (little kid lingo for being carried upstairs and put to bed) are dead! Get someone else to do it because it won't be me!" Got it?!

His bottom lip which had been protruding from pouting developed a tremulous quaver and I felt like the most horrible person on the face of the planet. I loved this little boy with all my heart and now he was on the verge of tears because of me. If only I could take my words back somehow. How could I be so ignorant? So thoughtless?

"I don't know what the hell your problem is little buddy." I said carefully --- soothingly, knowing damn well what his most immediate and current problem was. Me. I had just threatened to withhold my love and affection from a little kid who pretty much idolized me. He had no way of knowing that it was essentially hyperbole. He took his "hug all the way upstairs" very seriously. "I give you the best of everything. I even let you drive my car! <u>Only you.</u> Not even your mother drives my car. You have everything, **EVERYTHING** that a kid could want."

Tevon gave me a studied suspicious look which I recognized well from his mom, "I don't have everything that a kid could want. I don't have a <u>Super Soaker</u>."

"A Super Soaker! What's that?"

He closed my phone, handed it to me and said "take me to K-B Toys and I'll show you."

A half hour later when we exited the Toy Store, it was with two Super Soakers. When we got home, my wife kissed me and said, "I really wish you would stop smoking in the car when he is with you."

"Hi mom! Look, we got <u>Super Soakers</u>!" Tevon said brandishing his large capacity squirt gun.

"Tevon, I told you no <u>Super Soakers.</u>" My Wife scolded.

"Bob said it was okay." He smiled sweetly. The year is 2002.

---THE END---

TELLING THE TRUTH

I am a liar. Unlike most folks I'm not ashamed to admit I'm a compulsive liar, fetishitic fiber, and teller of tall tales. That's why I'm a professional writer; live me a bohemian lifestyle and I am almost unconcerned about the mundane, trivial things in life most folks preoccupy themselves with nowadays; like chasing a buck. I've got my priorities in order. Anyone can make money. Anyone can lie. Come to think of it, anyone can make money by lying.

Hell, I'd make a great insurance agent and an even better lawyer. But it would be fiscally irresponsible of me to just up and throw away my natural talent for fabrication like that. Besides having a beautiful soon-to-be pregnant future wife to consider I can't rightly see wasting perfectly good lies on folks who either don't deserve to be lied to or don't deserve to benefit from my aptitude for embellishment. I also prefer to work at home which has its perks and compensations believe you me; but this isn't about how gratifying my sex life is--- maybe some other time. Besides politics, what other field can you name where folks generously reward you for meeting their expectations of being a downright altruistic, clever, artful and ingenious liar? By the time I was ten year sold, I figured that the real difference between fiction and lies is the size of the paycheck and began honing my skills by studying the styles of great liars.

Being a writer is lonely work at times, especially when you've got a girlfriend who is a terrific liar herself like my Ginger is. "Oh honey, its wonderful." She gushed after reading my novel manuscript "The Paralegal". Is that so? Well if it so wonderful then why did she frown throughout the entire two and a half hours it took her to read it? For that matter, what woman, unless she's lying would think that a story with a graphically depicted, gruesome homosexual gang rape scene in a prison boiler room cumulating with a rapist being castrated by teeth is wonderful!? I knew darn tootin' that she was lying. Did I not sit right here in this wobbly chair at this very kitchen table in our $900 1973 30' Airstream Excello Travel Trailer examining her lover face for clue about her verdict while she read? By gosh I sure did. What about the illustrations? I say slyly putting her to the ultimate test. "They're really cute." Ginger beams.

Oh really? I snatch "The Paralegal" which Ginger is clutching protectively to her chest in a feeble attempt to prevent me from doing what she knows from prior experience is coming and commence to shred it. She is furious now too, but doesn't say a word. It's a good thing we're compatible and she understands me so well otherwise I wouldn't be half the liar I am.

When I sold my story "Kick Start" to Biking Viking Macho Man Magazine (my first big sale) last year for a whopping $25 ¼ a word making me $1500 richer it was Ginger who mixed the diamond engagement ring, wedding bands, civil ceremony and the fun-filled three day and two-night honeymoon in Las Vegas via junket. Like most young couples fresh out of high school and just starting off in life, we didn't have much to start with.

"If we get married on the money then we'll have to stay with your folks or mine." Ginger said . My people are poultry farmers and hers are in dairy products. "Your mom likes me and I want to keep it that way. Two women cannot share the same kitchen so we can't go to your folks. My pa will love having us both as slaves in exchange for our room and board. Cows are even worse than chickens, you'll never have time to write and we'll never have any privacy." She decided we wanted to be together in privacy and escape the drudgery and toil of farm life so we skipped the formalities in order to afford our own little love nest. Nobody much liked our decision but us.

For $900 and my '62 Olds Starfire for the trade in we got this trailer with a leaky roof and abused '70 International four-wheel drive pick-up truck with peeling imitation wood siding that grinds and sticks in second gear. We took a trip to Chicago where we purchased pre-owned wardrobes, bedding and stuff for the trailer from the Goodwill second hand store. Good sport that she is, Ginger acted like a kid at Christmas. You would've thought we were getting outfitted at Marshall Fields.

Come home from Chicago and found us a $300 check from Avengelical Press and a contract for 5% in royalties 'cause they want my story "Brothers of Destruction" for their anthology Profane Existence: Tales to Make your Skin Crawl. Ginger has her a genuine swoon.

The little woman wanted me to upgrade from the Big Chief writing tables to a fancy Smith Corona word processor with 75,000 word Spell mate and a 12-page editable memory that was on sale at Sears and sent me to go fetch one. As I crept along down U.S. Highway 41 at 30 miles per hour and ignored the angry honks, shaking fists, dirty looks and occasional middle finder from irritated motorists who zoomed past me while wrestling with the darned ole shifter (trying to get out of second) I said to heck with it. I have me an unabridged Oxford English Dictionary --- comes with two thick genuine leather bound volumes with a lil' magnifying glass 'cause its printed in double extra small ruin your vision type--- and four different thesauri. What in tarnation did I need Spell mate for?

The way I figured it, Big Chief was good enough for Johnboy Walton to write on so Big Chief will suffice for Trevor Thomas Twillman too; 'sides, I don't even know how to type 'cept by the Columbus method: search and land on it. Took myself in to the fella at the Happy Hocker pawnshop where I seen for myself what them balls on the sign out front was all about. "Ten-percent of the retail value and not a penny more." The friendly looking pawnbroker informed the long-haired dope smoker who wanted to hock his guitar. I got me a portable manual typewriter to learn on, a nice-sized chunk of rock and a Casio electronic keyboard ('cause I knew Ginger missed the old upright piano she had to leave behind at her mom's) for $515 plus tax. You should've seen the waterworks when I popped that ring on Ginger's finger.

Ginger just sets there with her arms crossed giving me the evil eye while I work on tearing "The Paralegal" into a million pieces. Like I said, she's a practical gal. I can tell by the color to her cheeks and the firm set to her jaw which makes her chin jut out that just as son as I've fulfilled my urge to destroy my creation she's going to light into me like an angry hornet and give me what for. Then the ole "You don't respect my opinion or trust my judgment" lecture when I'm plumb tuckered out from all the shredding, ripping and tearing. The stony silence makes me right uncomfortable so I keep my head down and decide to stave off the inevitable for as long as possible and concentrate on making them pieces real small. Pretty soon I've got me a good-sized mound of confetti going there.

"You best have my carbon copy of it Treavor Thomas Twillman or by golly…" Ginger snaps. "Do you? Answer me!" Yes'm" I mumble. Six months and three ripped-up manuscripts ago when Ginger stayed up all night long after sending me to bed with no supper (which was not all that much of a punishment as I wasn't particularly hungry now and I went to because I wanted to not 'cause she made me) and out of sheer bullheadedness painstakingly pierce my short story "Phony Smile" back together with scotch tape) she came up with a new rule; She gets a carbon copy of anything I write. She has lots of rules Ginger does. Like we always go to bed naked and we never go to sleep after a fight until we kiss and make up. Put the toilet seat down after use. Don't use an ink pen on the Sunday crossword puzzle. Rules a man can live with.

Ginger was especially vindicated when she sent a photocopy of "Phony (scotch taped together) Smile" to the literary journal Tevontronics and they sent us a $250 check for one-time rights which we got just in the nick of time to get us up to date on the back rent and forestall our eviction from Karr's Kampground and restock the empty larder. She was downright unfeeling when "Phony Smile" proved so bright it won the annual Tevontronics Short Story Contest for which we received an engraved silver bowl and $500. Her ego swelled so big it took up the whole trailer when the editor of Teveontrons nominated it for inclusion in the exclusive Flying Horses Short Fiction Literary Award. "Phony Smile" captivated and seduced the panel of judges. We won the much coveted four-foot tall flying Horse statue and five grand in prize money, beating the biggest names in the business. Adam Troy-Castro, Joyce Carol Oates and Stephen King included. Ginger never tires of telling me ---as if she's trying to make a strong point --- how if it weren't for wife Tabitha having the brains of the matches when she salvaged "Carrie" from the trash can, Stephen King would've never made good. As far as Ginger is concerned she won the silver bowl and the Flying Horse statue and I had nothing to do with it. Technically, she is correct.

As for that five grand in prize money, after we settle up with greedy ole Uncle Sam, at the first sign of cold weather it's good-bye Marquette, Michigan and hello Daytona Beach, Florida. The truck and trailer are getting some long overdue repairs. Ginger is getting some new clothes despite her protestations that she has enough to wear and I'm getting a tabletop photocopier. We're also getting hitched.

"Look at me when I'm talking to you Mr. Smarty-Pants." She fetches my head up by jerking a handful of hair. I know she's got her dander up. The first time she ever whupped me was in the third grade when I dropped an itty-bitty bullfrog down the front of her dress. Called me Mr. Smarty Pants and sent me home bawling for mom after she hung a mouse on me. "What have you got to say for yourself?"

I opened my soup-coolers to say what I've got to say for myself and she grabs a handful of confetti and throws it smack dab in my face. Not a bad throw for a girl, not bad at all. I can tell after knowing her all 19 years of her life, she's just warming up. I ain't made her this mad since the second time that she called me Mr. Smarty Pants five years ago over to the Freshman mixer at the high school. "Shut up." She commands.

There I sit doing as instructed with my very best Hangdog I'm sorry honeypie look wishing I was in hell to get away from her withering glare and hoping like hell she don't become afflicted with sudden loss of memory for her rules come bedtime. "You don't respect my opinion and you don't trust my judgment, " she says right mean-like. For some strange reason I get me a powerful urge to tell her I do so which was why I always sat next to her in seventh grade English. That way I could copy her answers in case of a pop-quiz. I get the idea she would think I'm trying to patronize her so I hold my tongue.

"You don't respect women at all you fat-headed male chauvinist pig!"

She stalks down to the 'bedroom' of our tandem-axle domicile and returned with the silver bowl she keeps on her nightstand ever since she took after me with the broom when she saw me us it for an ashtray. "Because of my opinion and judgment, you have this." She says brandishing it and points at the Flying Horse statue. And that. Now I want to know what in blue blazes made you tear up "The Paralegal" like you don't have the sense God gave a billy goat. Which you don't and don't you dare give me any of that sensitive writer nonsense like you did when you ripped up the "The Impasse" and its because I laughed you-you-you insensitive brute. I know darn well I wasn't laughing this time."

After spitting confetti from my tongue I splutter, "You lied to me!" "I lied to you? Are you crazy? We lie to each other all the time." I say this in a big breathless rush to get it all out before she takes it in mind to throw some more manuscript in my fae or break my nose like she did at Marquette High School. That happened at the dance when she called me Mr. Smarty Pants after I pinched her behind on a two dollar dare. Come to find out she really wasn't put out that I pinched her butt. She was mad 'cause I did it in front of everyone.

"We love each other." Ginger says slowly as if in shock. "I ain't never lied to you and I can't think of one time where you've lied to me. We ain't like them." She concludes by referring to my third cousin Tom and his wife Pattie who are both liars and cheaters of the lowest sort. "No we ain't like them." I agree. "I pray that we never will be. But we do lie to each other and it is because we love each other that we do so Gingerbread.

Her mouth turns up in just the teensiest hint of a smile. She likes it when I call her Gingerbread. I don't suppose the double -entendre escaped her when I told her the reason why. "Go on. I'm listening." No "Honey" in the sentence so I know she's still a mite upset with me. "Well you frowned the whole time you read it." "What does that have to do with lying?" "Look Ginger. When people are really and truly in love with each other –" "Like we are." She prompts gently. "Right. Like we are. When people are really and truly in love with each other like we are, they lie to each so that they don't hurt the other one's feelings. Which is exactly what we do all the time. If I wanted a biased opinion then I'd simply show the stories to my mom. She loves everything right down to the last punctuation error. I could see it in your face that you didn't like "The Paralegal" but you lied and said you did. Then you said the illustrations were cute which was an outrageous lie 'cause you know darn well I can't even draw an anatomically correct stickperson. That's why I got mad and tore it up. Take note: out of my total respect for women in general and adoration for you in particular I didn't resort to the sexist chauvinistic bias of standard rules of pronoun usage and instead applied the generic and gender-neutral term stickperson."

"Stop it!" Ginger giggles. "You ass." "I lie too Gingerbread so it's not a one-way street. When you changed hairstyles, I said I loved the new one to please you when I actually hated it. I also lied when you cut it short. I don't like it short like that. I wish you would grow it back the way it was before you started all these experiments and leave it alone. When you made that coconut cake a couple of weeks ago I lied about it too. You worked so hard on it and then kept hovering over me asking how I liked it so I knew it was important to you that I like it." "Hmmmph." Ginger snorts indignantly. "You ate five pieces in one sitting." "I was trying to be convincing baby. I told myself to eat five pieces even if it killed me. Anything less than my usual appetite would've made you suspicious." "Any other dislikes you've lied about? Honestly?" I tease. Ginger is smiling now. She gets up from her chair, sits on my lap and we hug.

"Yes." She says and brushes confetti from my hair. "I hate going over to your Uncle Bill and Aunt Wanda's to play Spades. I'm sick of Bill's wise cracks about me not having a regular job and Wanda's remarks about us being trailer trash living in sin. Especially when we ain't married yet and do live in a shabby trailer in a rundown trailer court masquerading as a campground. He can't even play Spades and always overbids his hand. Plus he has the disgusting habit of licking his warty fingers one by one after gobbling a handful of popcorn and then sticks his hand right back in the bowl!"

Ginger lays her head on my shoulder and snuggles close. "No more failures to communicate Trev and no more Friday nights at Aunt Wanda's – thank God. I hate going over there for the same reasons. I never said anything because I thought you enjoyed the outing and didn't want to spoil it for you. "Telling the truth is the new rule in the Twillman trailer. I want you to know I honestly do think "The

Paralegal" is wonderful! That's why I got so mad when you ripped it up. I was frowning because it kept me on the verge of tears from beginning to end. Trev we're going to be rich —mark my words --- it going to be a New Your Times bestseller!"

"What about the illustrations?" I say. "I said they were cute because they really are. I never said they were great." Ginger said and lifts her head up for a kiss. I kiss her and we sit in sinful domestic bliss. "Trev." Ginger says in a small voice. "Was it my cooking or the coconut you didn't like?" Taking her anxious face in both hand I kiss her again and again over and over. Then I look her directly in those soft brown imploring eyes that love everything I write. "The coconut." I lie without reservation.

---THE END---

THE ULTIMATUM

I loved my brother. I also loved my dog, my car and my girlfriend, Darlene's mom, Andrea. Okay, okay…that's a slight exaggeration. I did however, love Andrea's cooking and in my opinion that should count for something. Am I forgetting to mention someone? Darlene is an intentional omission. I did not love my girlfriend. How could I? She had a deep-seated pathological hatred for my car. My brother and my dog were on the top ten of her "shit list" too.

Darlene Grizelda Rybarczyk was a Polish Princess, a voluptuous hot "38-28-38" body with racy curves, which did not stop. She had an adorable face and a thimble-sized brain that had screeched to a halt when she reached puberty. Not only was she stupid, she was ignorant as well. One or the other, I probably could have contended with, but the two together presented a rather formidable combination, which I was ill-equipped to deal with at the tender age of 19 years.

The day I changed engines in my car is the day we broke up. The only thing different from the many other times we had broken up during the course of our stormy two-year relationship is that we called it quits for good. My brother, my dog, my car and the little girl who lived next door each played a peripheral role in the break up.

All I can say is thank God for obnoxious brothers, loyal dogs and cute little girls with pigtails. Rainy days are very conducive to ending relationships. Fortune smiled. On the day I swapped mills in my goat it rained. Darlene was in her Grizelda the "Wicked Bitch of the West" mode. The night before we had the usual viper-like viciously hissed and whispered spat in order to prevent her mom and step-dad from overhearing us fighting through the "paper thin" wall which separated their bedroom from ours. Ostensibly we were fighting about sex-she wanted to and I did not. You know the old saying about familiarity breeding contempt? In actuality we were fighting about everything and nothing. What fornication fails to cure, a good fight certainly will.

I had sworn to Andrea on my potential future son's life that her garage-which she had allowed me to borrow for a few weeks that somehow turned into over a year-would definitely be restored to her ownership by Saturday. I had two days to change engines and took note of the fact that her husband Sam failed to volunteer his services to help me. I reminded myself to keep it in mind the next time he needed me to perform another free-of-charge miracle on his rust bucket Buick that was weekly. His deuce and a quarter lived from paycheck to paycheck.

Saturday morning, I gave Dar a 15-minute Kwick-Lube (like motor vehicles, women require maintenance and become surly when they don't get it regularly) and out to the garage I went, all bright-eyed and bushy-tailed. As I crossed the backyard, lightning flashed, thunder rumbled ominously and an instant downpour erupted. Not the most auspicious way to begin a major undertaking.

Once in the garage, I turned on the lights, lifted up the overhead door and pulled the canvas tarp off of my baby: a 1968 Pontiac GTO convertible. As I said previously, Dar wasn't only stupid, but ignorant. She thought that the Subjugator (my brother's name for my car) was "ugly". The winner of the 1968 Motor Trend Car of the Year Award was one of-if-not-the most beautiful of all automobiles to ever roll off the assembly line and my prospective opinionated better half thought it was ugly. There's just no accounting for some people's tastes.

Admittedly, the Subjugator's curvaceous body was marred here and there with minor dings and dents accumulated over 19 years of parking lot skirmishes. True, the white mother-of-pearl paint job was so sun-faded that no amount of polishing and buffing would bring life back to the lusterless color, despite my Herculean efforts. One of the reasons I had determined to do nothing about the paint job was because Dar unctuously informed me with that perfect degree of snobbish pomposity required to incur my everlasting enmity, "I'm not riding in that ugly piece of junk until it's painted."

That suited me just fine. I wouldn't have to spring for a new set of seat-covers. As far as I was concerned the Subjugator would never be repainted. Ugly…Cars are like people: it's what's inside that really counts. What the Subjugator would possess after the engine swap was the mechanical equivalent of a pure heart of gold.

A $4,000.00 balanced and blue printed 1969 Pontiac Catalina 2+2 428 H.O. with stainless steel crank, billet aluminum connecting rods and pistons. It also contained a severe cam, ported and polished heads, massaged dual quad intake manifold with Carter AFB carbs and functional Ram Air. The chrome plating under the hood was blinding, as was the bill, which could have resolved the National Debt of any Third World Country. I confess! I didn't paint the car to spite Dar. I couldn't afford to have it painted.

My Shepard-Lab mix Trapper John, DOG (cute eh?) scratched on the side door of the garage. I let him in and got to work. I drained the antifreeze from the radiator into a huge pan I appropriated from Andrea's kitchen, disconnected the cooling line, and gave Trapper a boot in the ass when he went sniffing around the pan full of antifreeze. I pulled the upper and lower radiator hoses, disconnected the battery and removed the trick dual electric fans and radiator. I pulled the alternator and bracket and took off the wiring harness. I pulled the electric fuel pump.

No sooner had I slid under the car when Dar's five-year-old little brother, Sammy, and four-year-old, Shelly, the little girl who lived next door wandered in and gleefully announced that they intended to help me. Dar, who was supposed to be watching Sammy, had banished him from the house. You see what I mean? She was stupid and ignorant. The former because it was raining, yet she sent Sammy outside to play anyway. The latter because she knew damn well the kid would come into the garage and make a nuisance of himself when I didn't have the time to watch him. After admonishing the kids several times to leave Trapper alone, they were pulling his tail-and-threats of beating them only caused them to giggle and squeal with delight at the prospect. I appointed Shelly official radio monitor and Sammy chief tool handler. Trapper's huge pink tongue lolled out of the side of his mouth and he thumped his bushy tail in ardent approval of my decision.

I slid back beneath the Subjugator which rested open four sturdy jack stands and pulled the bolts out of the motor mounts, dropped the starter, unbolted the transmission mount and disconnected the speedometer cable, reverse light switch and shifter linkage. Removed the drive shaft. Dragged the floor jack under the car, placed a piece of scrap 2 x4 lumber on the pad (to prevent the costly finned aluminum pan from being damaged) and jacked the Turbo 400 up. I then pumped the tranny up an inch of so and pulled the bolts out of the cross member free. Then I removed the 2 ½" stainless steel exhausts piped (with cutouts!) from the chrome-plated headers. When I crawled out from under the car I was covered with dirt and grime from head to toe.

Having been hard at it for several hours, I was somewhat annoyed that my brother. Tom hadn't shown up. I sent Sammy to the house with instructions to tell Dar to call Tom to see if he was going to honor his promise to come over and help me change engines (in lieu of the $250.00 bucks, which he had borrowed from me with no intention of ever repaying). I also asked him to find out what was for lunch. When Sammy returned, he informed me that Dar said Tom had called and would be over in a little while and she didn't answer him about lunch. See what I mean? Sheer ignorance. She didn't even have the common civil courtesy to come out and tell me that my brother had called and there I was doing her job of babysitting her kid brother: on an empty stomach!

I pulled the hood off by myself-which was a piece of cake-as it was a very expensive and relatively lightweight aftermarket fiberglass job. I assembled the rented engine crane, removed both carbs and bolted the crane chains to the intake manifold. After making my helpers stand clear, pulled the brutal 400 Ram Air IV engine which had done me justice innumerable times on Diversey Avenue; hence the name Subjugator my brother had expertly bestowed with an airbrush on the trunk deck spoiler. I busied myself removing all of the chrome plated engine dress up accessories from the 400 which would go on the 428 and were a major source of contention between Dar and I due to the cost which had set me back more funds than I care to discuss...

Dar put in an appearance as I was in the process of removing the 428 from the shopping cart it sat on (which I had stolen from a Jewel's store parking lot and converted into a make shift engine stand with my trusty hacksaw) and replacing it with the 400. She slapped a paper plate with potato chips and Spam sandwiches down on the fender of the Subjugator. One look at her scowling face, I decided on the spot that discretion was in fact the better part of valor. She knew I detested Spam. The witch. Instead, I asked, "What about something to eat for the kids?"

Dar eyed the children, who looked at her expectantly-both whom I noticed for the first time had somehow managed to get themselves and their clothing quite dirty in an amazingly brief period of time. With considerable distaste, she coldly said "this is not a restaurant and I am not a waitress. Sammy can go in the house and feed himself and Shelly can go home to eat."

I'm no ambassador, but I made a sincere attempt to be diplomatic and reasonable. "look Dar—"

"Look nothing!" Dar fumed. "I've about had it with you! How much do you think I can tolerate? You know I don't want your jag off brother around here after what he did to me, but you go ahead and invite him over anyway.

You were supposed to be watching Sammy! How did he get so dirty? We know who's got to clean him up. Me! That's Who!

Your performance this morning left a lot to be desired! Don Juan you aren't [SNEER]. Instead of saving your money for our wedding, you spend it all on tools and car parts for this piece of junk. Don't you realize I'm the best thing that ever happened to you? Answer me damn you!"

"Darlene-" I said through gritted teeth.

"Don't you dare interrupt me when I'm speaking to you

Frank."

She spotted the pan of antifreeze I had placed on top of the workbench to keep out of Trapper's reach. "Well we know where mother's roaster disappeared. Make sure that you replace it with a new one: today! If it weren't for my mother you wouldn't even have a place to stay. Furthermore----"

Little Shelly who along with Sammy had been clinging to and cowering behind my legs while Dar delivered her "Wicked Bitch of the West" impersonation darted out from behind me and shouted indignantly, "You leave Frank alone you big meany!" and landed what appeared to be a pretty powerful kick (for a four-year-old anyway) to Dar's shin.

"Ooohh you rotten brat!" Dar cried and grabbed Shelly by the arm and swatted her on the rump. At this point, I interjected myself into a classic example of egregious abuse of power by seizing Dar's wrist in mid-swing as she went to apply her hand to Shelly's backside.

"Let go of me this instant!" Dar demanded and struggled ineffectually against my grasp.

I fixed her with my sternest glare "Stop it!" She whimpered. "You're hurting me.

I relaxed my grip somewhat and let go of some pent-up bitter invective. "First of all, you were supposed to watch Sammy, not me.

I'm supposed to get this engine swap done so that Andrea can get her garage back by tomorrow. Sammy got dirty cause this is a garage, not a nursery school."

Secondly, I do appreciate everything that Andrea has done for me. I could've moved in with Tom and therefore would have a place to live, but you wanted me to move in with you. And let's not lose sight of the fact that I pay $50.00 bucks a week to live here so I can listen to Sam comment about how much I eat; and work on his car without compensation.

Thirdly, I never claimed to be 'Don Juan', if my performance doesn't meet your high standard why is it that you want to get married to me? What's with your big rush to get to the altar anyway? You don't look pregnant to me. If and when we do get married this car is going to pay for the wedding one way or another. Now get your lazy ass in the kitchen and fix lunch for the kids and bring me something else to eat besides Spam!"

"I'm telling mother!" She sobbed.

"Go right ahead! Just make sure you don't neglect to tell her that you sent Sammy out to play in the rain and that you abused Shelly. I'm sure she'll be real proud of you when I tell her about your actions."

Darlene flounced out of the garage and Sammy trailed along dejectedly behind her when she ordered him to the house. I picked Shelly up off the floor as she was crying hard enough to make my heart burst. She wrapped her arms around my neck and said, "I'm sorry for being bad."

I told her, "Honey, you're the best radio monitor I ever had and if you don't stop crying, I'm going to cry too and well we'll both look silly."

"Really?" She sniffled.

"Cross my heart, hope to die, stick a needle in my eye." I solemnly vowed.

I wiped her tears away. "When we're done fixing the car I'm going to get you the nicest doll you ever saw for being such a big help." Hell, that kick to Dar's shin was the price of ten dolls. I put her back on the ground and she looked up at me speechless with huge shining eyes.

Shelly had lived a hard life for one so young. At age three, her old man had come home after a hard night of barhopping, smacked her bimbo of a mom around (who protected him at the expense of Shelly being abused). Then he beat the poor kid bad enough to put her in Belmont Community Hospital's Charity Ward for two months. Tom, our cousin Jack (who was Tom's partner in high profit adventures) and myself ran into the pezzo di merda one night outside of an after-hours joint in Cicero (town outside of Chicago). I worked him over pretty good when you take into consideration that I'm a firm believer in nonviolence. Tom and Jack had to pull me off of him for fear I would make good on my threats to kill him. Then,

Tom told the bastard he wouldn't have to worry about me if he put his hands on Shelly again. He kicked him dead straight in the mouth twice for emphasis with steel-toed engineer boot clad feet which sent teeth flying everywhere. Unlike me, Tom greatly enjoys gratuitous violence, especially when he is the party inflicting it on others. Her Dad left Chicago.

Darlene returned carrying a plate full of peanut butter and jelly sandwiches. Service with a snarl. Sammy bore a brimming pitcher of Kool-Aid and paper cups. Before I even had a chance to thank her, she stormed out of the garage thundering dark imprecations about the bleak things in store for me once she reported me to the proper governmental agency for violating the child labor laws. We all three stuck out our tongues and made faces behind her back after she slammed the door shut behind her. This sent the kids into peals of laughter and suddenly a diffident 19-year-old for the first time soberly questioned himself as to whether he really wanted to continue on with a spoiled and selfish woman who not only loathed virtually everyone and everything he cared about, but hated children as well.

Tom pulled up in the alley on his customized '59 Harley-Davidson with his current flame LaTisha, a strapped up Oakie airhead built like a brick 'you know what' sitting behind him. I threw Trapper one of the Spam sandwiches he was eyeing lustfully which he demolished with a snap and a gulp. His tail beat out a rapid staccato on the floor as he looked at me incredulously as if to say 'that's it?'

Tom and LaTisha came into the garage and I gave them the condensed version of the latest episode in my ongoing feud with Darlene, which caused Tom to snort derisively. LaTisha wanted to go shopping so I let her borrow my daily driver, a stock '70 Mercury Cyclone and gave her $50.00 to pick up a doll for Shelly and a Tonka truck that I happened to know that Sammy desperately wanted. It had stopped raining earlier and the kids quickly lost their enthusiasm to help me, and went into the back yard to play with Trapper.

Just a few words to mention about my big brother. He is five years older than me, had easily ten grand worth of tattoos blanketing his neck, arms, back and stomach, and is a graduate of the "School of Hard Knocks" with an advanced degree in Thuggery. Tom has practiced all of the felonious trades and has a hard face, a hard attitude and a hard stomach. He got hard like that doing seven years in and out of the "Big House' at Joliet. Mostly in. Women are irresistibly drawn to him like moths to a light; he knows it and takes full advantage of it. With the exception of one girlfriend who shall remain nameless (she knows who she is), Tom has sampled the charms of all of my girlfriends-mostly during my relationships with them. He does not, however, comprehend that he is doing me a great injustice. To the contrary, he literally believes he is discharging his fraternal duty by ensuring that my girlfriends are good enough for me.

About six months before the "Great Engine" swap, Tom and

Dar came out to the garage where I was busy installing new polyurethane upper and lower control arm bushings in the Subjugator. As soon as I saw them together I knew the score. I would've known even if Dar hadn't been clinging to his arm like a blood sucking leach. They informed me that they were truly sorry, they had not intended for it to happen and it wasn't their intent to hurt me. They were in love. Evidently, they mistook the tears in my eyes for sorrow. Two weeks later she was back with a spectacular looking black eye and puffy lip. What happened was Dar could not accept Tom's philandering and assaulted him, seizing that part of his person mentioned by Moses in Deuteronomy 25:11 causing him such anguish as to subsequent conduct. She insisted I move in with her. Like a fool I did and with the gall and audacity commonly found among women of her stripe, She made my life miserable by subjecting me to vexatious harangues about what Tom had done to her as though she was the injured party.

It took us a couple of hours to bolt the Subjugator together. Tom took her for a test drive to the grocery store to pick up a new roaster for Andrea, while I erased all evidence of goat habitation from her garage, except for the 400 which Andrea's brother Steven was going to pay me $600.00 for. I heard Darlene shriek like a banshee and then Trapper raced through the side door of the garage hell bent for leather, out the overhead door and down the alley yipping happily. Tom pulled into the garage grinning broadly and waving the speeding ticket he had caught, as Dar came barreling through the side door brandishing a tree limb in hot pursuit of the dog.

"Where is he?" she demanded.

"Where is who?" Tom and I asked in unison.

"Don't talk to me jerk." She directed at Tom.

"Call me a jerk again and you'll be weeping." Tom warned as he disarmed her.

"Frank don't you just stand there and let him talk to me like that!"

"What do you want him to do about it?" Tom asked.

"Darlene what is the problem?" I asked annoyed.

"The problem is that four-footed fleabag of yours peed on my leg!" She yelled.

I digested this information. Dar's hatred of Trapper was longstanding. It was a case of hate at first sight. He certainly hadn't helped matters by singling out her new shoes for the ones he just had to chew on. She also despised the fact that I talked to him more than I talked to her, yet conveniently overlooked another fact: she never shut up long enough for me to get a word in edgewise. Then too, there was the little matter that while she was so stupid she didn't know the difference between a 7/16" open end wrench and a ½" box end wrench, Trapper did, as I had him demonstrate in order to prove that he was not "a dumb mutt".

"Peed on your leg?" I ventured tentatively.

"That's right!" She snapped, "I was in the chaise lounge

watching Sammy and Shelly while they were in the wading pool and "Crapper" came sniffing around by my feet. I made him go away. Then he came back while I was looking at a magazine. He lifted his leg and peed on mine!" Tom and I looked at each other and burst into laughter.

"Stop laughing! It's not funny!" Dar said growing angrier the harder we laughed.

But we laughed even harder.

Darlene stomped her feet in anger. Lucky for me Tom was right there or she would have undoubtedly attacked me. Trapper slunk into the garage on his belly and covered behind my legs.

"It's either the damn dog or me!" Dar shouted pointing at Trapper. "Make up your mind right now!"

I looked at Darlene who assumed a combative stance with hands on her hips glaring fiercely at me. I looked at Tom who turned away in utter disgust, ashamed that I was his flesh and blood. Then I looked down at man's best friend who looked at me with trust and whined softly. I opened the driver's door of the Subjugator and shoed Trapper into the back seat. "I'll be back later to get my clothes."

"I knew you liked him better than me" she accused. "If you leave me, how am I going to get to work on Monday?"

Darlene didn't drive. She was too stupid to pass the road test.

"On this!" I said and thrust the broom I had been sweeping the floor with into her hands.

---THE END---

TOOTHILY YOURS

How do you make a 6'1" 180 lb. Union Ironworker holler in humiliating hurt and agony? It's really quite simple: the exact same way you would to any other red-blooded American male. Have a six-year-old boy affix a mouthful of molars to a digit and exert extreme jaw pressure. Mind you… I did not scream as that would be most undignified --- not to mention unmanly. I prefer the term <u>yowled</u> as the most accurate depiction of the event.

That Sunday morning --- like every Sunday morning --- I was the only one dressed and ready for Church. Which was fine with me. Sunday was all about rituals, traditions and [ahem] <u>observance.</u> When my wife realized that I was perfectly content to stand in our bathroom doorway and ogle her scantily clad backside as she stood half-dressed before the vanity mirror expertly applying make up to (what to my mind was) a perfect, unblemished and gorgeous face, she grew perturbed with my voyeurism. She was saucy, sassy and sexy. I thoroughly enjoyed watching the meticulous and mysterious process of transformation; the mindboggling metamorphosis from smart and stylish social worker to sensuous and smoldering supermodel.

I loved my wife. I never tired of the unintended quasi-burlesque show which frankly was amazing and a great way to kill time. Her annoyance was because I could not restrain myself from interfering with the process by way of lascivious caresses, gropes, pats and pinches. My participation was not included as part of her protocol, so wielding a hot curling iron she banished me from her threshold. "Now quit!" She ordered. "Go away. Make sure Tevon is dressed and eats. I'll be ready to go in 10 minutes."

Glumly I nodded my assent. For the most part, she had me mastered, hence my acquiescence in most matters but smoking. However, one thing which she had never completely mastered was how to properly tell time. Her "ready to go in 10 minutes" was actually Wife Time which entailed a basic working knowledge of quantum mechanics to adequately decipher. I possessed such arcane knowledge which was why I was such a formidable JEOPARDY! opponent. She meant I had a half an hour to go. I departed very quickly after one final pinch to her decorous derriere and went downstairs.

My stepson Tevon was parked in front of the TV eating a bowl of Fruit Loops and wearing nothing but his Power Rangers underoos. He was for the most part very well-behaved and low maintenance. He was a blessing in my life and an only child. He got blessed a lot. My wife would frequently lecture me about spoiling him, which I freely admit I did --- because I could not help myself. Between us we had quite a sizeable joint income. We could afford to be generous and bestow the best of everything on our little boy. And I loved him and wanted him to love me. Tevon was a diehard Power Rangers fan and had Power Rangers everything. You name it.

"Finish that up and go get dressed little Buddy." I said taking a page from my wife's playbook. "We're leaving in 10 minutes."

I slipped out the back door and went out to the garage. Normally, I would have been much stealthier and more secretive, if not downright sneaky. Smoking was <u>verboten</u>. My wife and her extra set of eyes and ears ~ yes: Tevon was a trained informant ~ were both busy making preparations to leave, so I was safe to indulge. I fired up an unfiltered Lucky Strike and set about putting a truly high-gloss luster on my wingtips with the disposable Armor All wipes bolstered with a shot of aerosol spray WD-40. Perfect mirror finish every time. Plus the WD40 masked the smoke. Once back in the house, I observed two things. First, only 10 minutes had passed. Second, Tevon was now heavily engaged in a Transformers cartoon and still was not dressed. I adopted a firmer tone, "Hey, I said get upstairs and get dressed."

He ignored me. The telephone rang and My wife's voice floated downstairs for me to answer the phone, which I did. I spent a good 8 minutes talking to my lackey Keith—(long story about him some other time) about the work I planned to do on my 1969 T-Bird 2 door hard top. My pride and joy -after My wife mind you. Cleaning up, I noticed that my little Buddy still had not troubled to dress himself. "I told you to go upstairs and get dressed!" I said crossly.

Every once in a while I had to get stern because Tevon decided that not only did he not have to listen to me but that he would not listen to me. This apparently was on of those times. The last time we went through this phase of his character development and deportment he stuck his tongue out at my wife and I. Disobedience and disrespect were of course unacceptable. Lesson learned when mom vigorously applied the wooden spoon to his bottom. This time he had determined to disregard me completely. I was left to deal with this insurrection on my own. So I did.

"You're going to church just like that." I said snatching him up with grim decisiveness. The sudden and severe pain which immediately followed was indescribable. There is absolutely <u>nothing</u> so unbelievably excruciating as 50 lbs., of teeth ferociously attached to the tip of your thumb with the dedicated tenacity of a pit bull. The truth of the matter is: I wailed like a banshee --- long and loud. Very loud. Our dog Daisy joined in the cacophonous chorus yelping and yipping when I inadvertently trod on her tail as I danced about shrieking in agony trying to shake him off.

For a little kid he delivered an impressive amount of pressure per square inch. I gave him a healthy slap which caused him to relinquish his toothy death grip and his cries were added to that of mine and the dog. "What on earth is going on in there?" My wife shrieked. "He bit me! He [expletives deleted] bit me!" I ranted furiously. "Well bite him back!" she bellowed.

"Great idea Honey Bunny!" I said grabbing Tevon who tried to squirm away. But I was too quick for him. I grabbed his arm and sank my teeth down into his gamey flesh. Time you had a bath Spunky! I thought maliciously. His screams were music to my ears!

My wife came down the stairs and stood in the center of the living room, hands on her hips and glared at her progeny. "I can't leave you alone for two minutes without you getting into some mischief."

Talk about adding insult to injury. **'Two minutes?'** **'Mischief?'** My wife's concept of reality was as distorted as her sense of time! "You know what my old man would've done to me if I would've ever bit him?!" I raved outraged. She knew. Her face was full of worry and concern.

"I would be an edentate! I would not have a [EXPLETIVE DELETED] tooth in my head!" I slammed out the front door and stood on the front stoop. In my fury I did not attempt to conceal the fact that once again I had resumed my filthy habit of smoking by openly lighting up. Through the screen door behind me I could hear my wife and Tevon talking in the living room. "Tevon what on earth possessed you to bite Bob?"

"Well", he sniffled through his tears, "He said I had to go to church just like this because I didn't get up and get dressed. When he picked me up I knew if I bit him he would have to let me go." "Did you like it when Bob bit you back?" My wife asked.

"No Mama." Tevon said mournfully. "Bob's bite is worse than his bark." My thumb throbbed dully. Rivulets of blood seeped through several puncture wounds. I could not help but laugh ruefully. I could say the same about him.

---THE END---

WHAT IS NORMAL?

Orange Really Is the New Black. Abandonment. Neglect.
Being unloved and unwanted. Being hated and despised. To be
forgotten. The void in my soul. The total inability to ever trust
another human being again.

The complete lack of capacity in others to say what they
mean and mean what they say. Low lifes. Scumbags. Backstabbing.
Deceit. Treachery. Two-bit punks emboldened by their penitentiary
tattoos somehow elevated to major league crime boss or baller status
~ to hear them tell it ~ because mom provides the money for a new
pair of sneakers. Betrayal. Empty eyes and empty smiles. Insincerity.
False Gods and False Religions.

False remedies in the form of color TV and medication. A
man's word being worthless. Sodomy. Homosexuals, Bisexuals and
Transsexuals. Shamelessness. Shallow solutions and perverted
placeboes. The deficit of dignity and squandering of self-respect.
Child molesters housed safely in general population. Aggravation,
stagnation and isolation. Being apart from others. Being ready to
descend upon the next motherfucker like the Wrath of God at the
slightest provocation with no hesitation or mercy.

A profane existence. A new generation with no standards,

morals or values. An aura of violence. An era of hatred. Cowards upgraded to Gangsters and Gangsters reduced to bywords. The stony feeling in my heart. Concrete, steel and razor wire. Guards armed with tasers. Gangs. Groups. Organizations. Avarice. Going to bed hungry. Waking up hungrier. Not receiving any mail. Profane thoughts. Sinister wisdom. Sensory deprivation. Pepper spray panaceas.

Looking back at my distorted reflection in the polished metal plate bolted to the wall. <u>Knowing</u> that the Big House is not a Fun House or a rite of passage to manhood. Truly wondering if my thoughts are as distorted as the wavy image of the gray-haired man staring back at me.

---THE END---

ABOUT THE AUTHOR

Robert F. Nelson, Jr., known by his family and friends as *Bobby* and in the field as *Bob*, is a product of his personal philosophy: "UBU IBME." "You Be You; I Be Me" is an epithet that consistently rings true of how he sees and interacts with people. During the course of in his life time he has seen people at their worst and best. His goal is useful conversation; not to change others but to share some level of useful wisdom and knowledge to serve as a companion to their journey.

For more than 30 years, Bobby, has been a Union Iron Worker, spending his seasons in most of the 50 states on assignment and following the growth of the urban and suburban Metropolis. No stranger to hard work and life on the edge, Bobby's command of the English language, trivia and history might surprise even the brightest erudite.

Nelson, has stores of writings in his archives, waiting to be shared in books, movies and on stage. Many of his collections were formed in the quiet moments of confinement when his thoughts and imagination were unleashed. Other works were formed through his life-lessons at the peak of his moments of awakening. Always underestimated, this published writer still has an unlimited amount of literary acumen to spare.

Like the stories?

Want to share your feedback?

Reach out to me at:

Robertfnelsonjr23@gmail.com

www.ingramcontent.com/pod-product-compliance
Lightning Source LLC
Chambersburg PA
CBHW050414030726
47503CB00006B/2181